D1425714

RSPB wild
nature
COLOURING book

A & C BLACK
AN IMPRINT OF BLOOMSBURY
LONDON NEW DELHI NEW YORK SYDNEY

Published 2013 by
A&C Black, an imprint of Bloomsbury Publishing Plc
50 Bedford Square, London, WC1B 3DP

www.bloomsbury.com

ISBN 978-1-4081-9249-8

A CIP catalogue for this book is available from the British Library.

Every effort has been made to trace copyright holders and to obtain their
permission for use of copyright material. The author and publishers would be
pleased to rectify any error or omission in future editions.

This book is produced using paper that is made from wood grown in managed,
sustainable forests. It is natural, renewable and recyclable. The logging and
manufacturing processes conform to the environmental regulations of the
country of origin.

Produced for Bloomsbury Publishing by Calcium. www.calciumcreative.co.uk

Illustrations © Carol Jonas, Robin Bouttell, Ian Jackson, Sandra Pond,
Peter Scott 2012
Cover illustrations © Robin Bouttell, Carol Jonas 2012

Printed in China by C & C Offset Printing Co., Ltd.

All the internet addresses given in this book were correct at the time of going to
press. The author and publishers regret any inconvenience caused if addresses
have changed or sites have ceased to exist, but can accept no responsibility
for any such changes.

10 9 8 7 6 5 4 3 2 1

Contents

Wild nature

When you're out and about on your wildlife adventures you will see lots of amazing things. From beautiful birds hunting for food to night-time bats and badgers, and even shells at the seashore, nature is everywhere!

In this book you will find 35 common wild nature creatures and plants to colour in as well as beautiful illustrations to copy, amazing wildlife facts and even a spotter's guide so you can tick off what you've seen!

Red squirrel

Red squirrels have orange coloured fur with white fronts and bushy tails. This red squirrel is holding a pine cone.

Fallow deer

This fallow deer is brown with white spots. But fallow deer can also be plain brown, black or white.

 # Rabbit

This rabbit has
brown-grey fur
with a white tail.
Rabbits live
in burrows.

Harvest mouse

The harvest mouse is really small. But it has a very long tail!

Water shrew

Water shrews
have black hairs
on their back
and silvery hairs
on their fronts.
They are brilliant
swimmers!

Stoat

A stoat's fur can turn white in the winter. But its tail-tip stays black.

Elephant hawkmoth

You are most likely to see this pretty green and pink moth at night when it comes out to find nectar to drink.

Purple hairstreak butterfly

This purple butterfly is licking the sticky honeydew from the leaf it sits on.

Gatekeeper butterfly

This orange and brown butterfly is also called a hedge brown. Can you see the tiny white spots on its back wings?

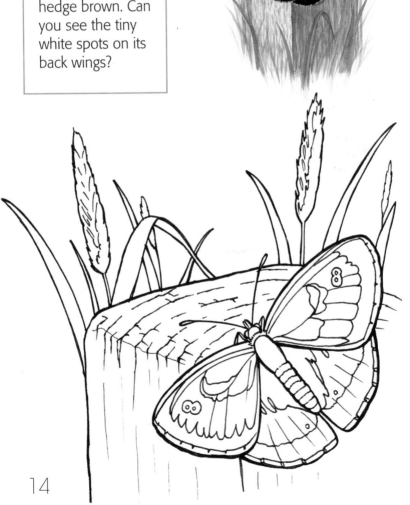

Peacock butterfly

Look at the
patterns on the
wings of this
beautiful butterfly.
They look just
like the eyes in
a peacock's tail!

Common daisy

These yellow
and white
flowers open
in the daytime.
Then they close
at night!

Bluebell

These blue flowers look like tiny bells. Their leaves are thin and shiny.

Yellow iris

Yellow irises are often found by water. They have thick lines down the middle of their leaves.

Spruce cones

These cones are found on spruce trees. Your Christmas tree is probably a spruce tree.

Horse chestnut

Horse chestnut trees grow prickly nuts like these. People call the nuts conkers.

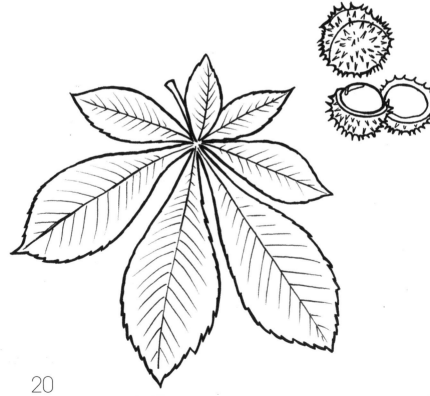

Emperor dragonfly

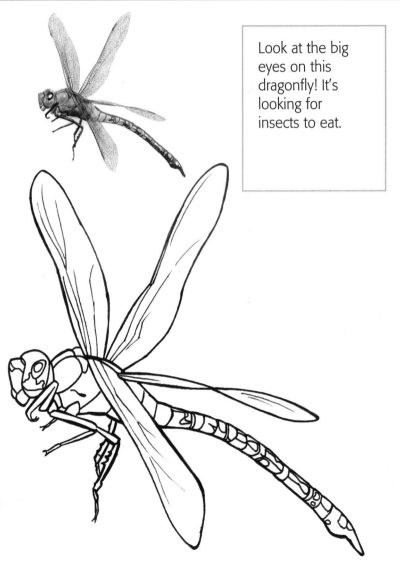

Look at the big eyes on this dragonfly! It's looking for insects to eat.

Heron

These grey birds can be found near water looking for fish and frogs to eat.

Stickleback

This male stickleback has a red patch underneath its belly. Females are silver underneath.

Grass snake

This green, black and white snake is the largest snake in Britain. It has grey and white markings underneath.

Common toad

Look at the
bumps on this
toad's skin.
This is how you
can tell it apart
from a frog.

Smooth newt

Colourful smooth newts live in and around ponds. Male newts have orange and red tummies.

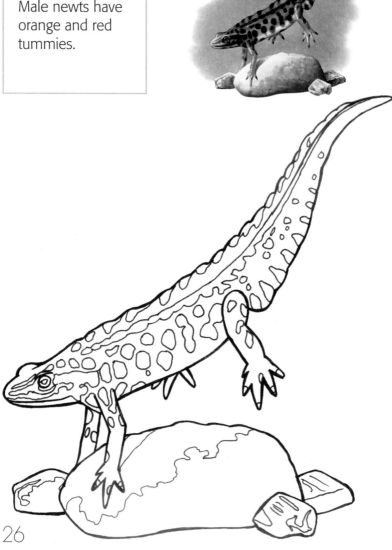

Starfish

A starfish can be found at the seashore. Its mouth is underneath its body!

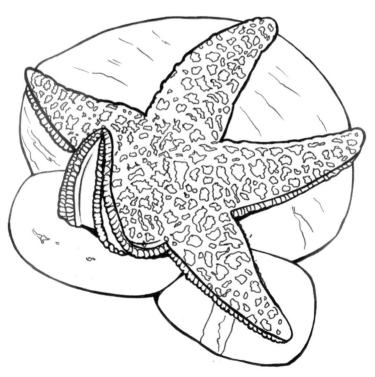

Anemone

This sea creature uses its tentacles to sting. But it hides them away when the tide goes out.

Sea urchin

Sea urchins that are alive have prickly spines. The round shell on this page is just the sea urchin's skeleton.

Butterfish

This fish gets its name because it's a slippery fish not because it's yellow like butter.

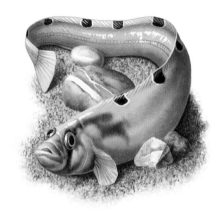

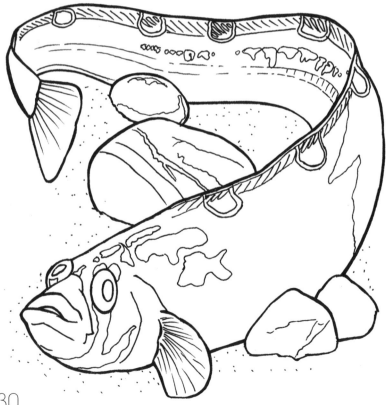

Shore crab

This seashore creature has big claws for catching food to eat. Can you see its eyes on the end of their stalks?

Whelk

A whelk lives by
the sea. It uses
the tube coming
out of its shell
to drill holes into
other shells to
find its dinner!

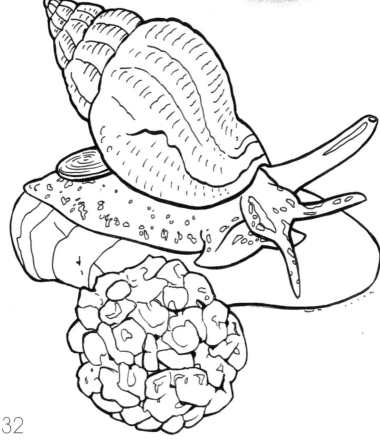

Buzzard

This large bird has a short tail and very broad wings. It is the most common bird of prey in the UK.

 # Great tit

This colourful bird has a yellow front but a green back. Can you also see the black stripe that runs down its front?

Mallard

Female and male mallards look very different from one another. The male has a green head. Females are mostly brown.

Barn owl

These pretty birds
are mainly seen at
night. When they
catch something
to eat they
swallow it whole!

Kingfisher

Kingfishers have
striking blue and
orange feathers
like this one. A
female kingfisher
even has orange
on her beak.

Great spotted woodpecker

This bird lives in the woods. Only the male has a red spot on the back of its head.

Swallow

You can't always see it because they're so fast but swallows have a red patch on their throats and on their heads.

39

Herring gull

These seaside birds have a red spot on their beaks. Can you see it?

Spotter's guide

How many of these things have you seen on your wildlife adventures? Tick them when you spot them.

Red squirrel
page 6

Fallow deer
page 7

Rabbit
page 8

Harvest mouse
page 9

Water shrew
page 10

41

Stoat
page 11

Elephant hawkmoth
page 12

Purple hairstreak butterfly
page 13

Gatekeeper butterfly
page 14

Peacock butterfly
page 15

Common daisy
page 16

Bluebell
page 17

Yellow iris
page 18

Spruce cones
page 19

Horse chestnut
page 20

Emperor
dragonfly
page 21

Heron
page 22

Stickleback
page 23

Grass snake
page 24

Common toad
page 25

Smooth newt
page 26

Starfish
page 27

Anemone
page 28

Sea urchin
page 29

Butterfish
page 30

Shore crab
page 31

Whelk
page 32

Buzzard
page 33

Great tit
page 34

Mallard
page 35

Barn owl
page 36

Kingfisher
page 37

Great spotted
woodpecker
page 38

Swallow
page 39

Herring gull
page 40

Find out more

If you have enjoyed
this colouring book and
would like to find out
more about wildlife
you might like RSPB Wildlife Explorers.

Visit www.rspb.org.uk/youth
to find lots of things to
make and do, and
to play brilliant
wildlife games.

If you like learning about nature you might also like this RSPB book:

HB 978-1-4081-7888-1
PB 978-1-4081-7889-8